MR.CHEERFUL

MR. CHEERFUL

by Roger Hargreaves

Mr Cheerful always woke up in a
cheerful mood, with a bright
sunny smile on his face.

In fact Mr Cheerful was one of the most
cheerful people you are ever likely to meet.

He did, however, have one secret
that made him sad,
but nobody knew about it.

Not yet, anyway.

All I can tell you is that he liked to
keep it under his hat.

Mr Cheerful was never without a smile.

From breakfast time in the morning...

... to his bath time at night,
Mr Cheerful beamed from ear to ear.

He was even happy when it rained.

And on a sunny day,
his smile was even brighter and sunnier
than the sun.

Everybody around him couldn't help
but feel cheerful.

Even the flowers smiled when Mr Cheerful walked past.

When Mr Funny met him, he felt so happy
that he pulled an even
funnier face than usual,
making Mr Cheerful laugh out loud.

Then one day, while out for a walk,
Mr Cheerful bumped into Little Miss Splendid.

Mr Cheerful smiled his usual cheerful smile.

Little Miss Splendid began to smile,
but then she stopped, and looked sternly
at Mr Cheerful.

"How rude!" she exclaimed.
"Young man, don't you know
that you should raise your hat
when you meet a lady!"

For the first time in his life
Mr Cheerful lost his smile.

And then he blushed, bright red!

But he still did not raise his hat.

"You should be ashamed of yourself!"
cried Little Miss Splendid.
"Why won't you raise your hat?"

"I'm too embarrassed," replied Mr Cheerful,
blushing an even brighter red.
"Without my hat on I'm not very good-looking
and that makes me sad."

"Really?" asked Little Miss Splendid.
"Let me see."

Mr Cheerful lifted his hat.

And now I'll tell you what his secret was.

Mr Cheerful had a grand total
of only three hairs on his head!

"Is that all you're worried about?"
asked Little Miss Splendid.
"Why, it's your bright sunny smile
that everybody loves, not how many hairs
you have on your head!"

And Little Miss Splendid smiled.

Then Mr Cheerful smiled.

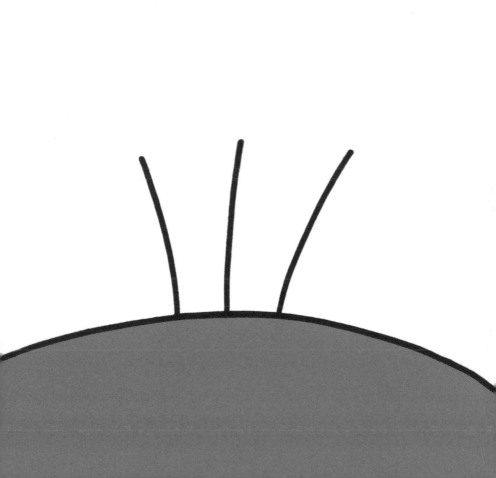

And ever since that day
he hasn't stopped smiling.

And he is always quick to raise his hat

to everyone he meets.

And everyone he meets goes away
feeling happy and cheerful.

Which leaves only one thing
left to say ...

... hats off to Mr Cheerful!

Fantastic offers for Mr. Men fans!

Collect all your Mr. Men or Little Miss books in these superb durable collectors' cases!

Only £5.99 inc. postage and packing, these wipe-clean, hard-wearing cases will give all your Mr. Men or Little Miss books a beautiful new home!

Keep track of your collection with this giant-sized double-sided Mr. Men and Little Miss Collectors' poster.

Collect 6 tokens and we will send you a brilliant giant-sized double-sided collectors' poster! Simply tape a £1 coin to cover postage and packaging in the space provided and fill out the form overleaf.

Only need a few Mr. Men or Little Miss to complete your set? You can order any of the titles on the back of the books from our Mr. Men order line on 0870 787 1724. Orders should be delivered between 5 and 7 working days.

— **TO BE COMPLETED BY AN ADULT** —

To apply for any of these great offers, ask an adult to complete the details below and send this whole page with the appropriate payment and tokens, to: MR. MEN CLASSIC OFFER, PO BOX 715, HORSHAM RH12 5WG

☐ Please send me a giant-sized double-sided collectors' poster.
AND ☐ I enclose 6 tokens and have taped a £1 coin to the other side of this page.

☐ Please send me ☐ Mr. Men Library case(s) and/or ☐ Little Miss library case(s) at £5.99 each inc P&P

☐ I enclose a cheque/postal order payable to Egmont UK Limited for £............................

OR ☐ Please debit my MasterCard / Visa / Maestro / Delta account (delete as appropriate) for £............................

Card no. ☐☐☐☐☐☐☐☐☐☐☐☐☐☐☐☐☐☐☐☐   Security code ☐☐☐

Issue no. (if available) ☐   Start Date ☐☐/☐☐/☐☐   Expiry Date ☐☐/☐☐/☐☐

Fan's name: ....   Date of birth: ....

Address: ....

....

....   Postcode: ....

Name of parent / guardian: ....

Email for parent / guardian: ....

Signature of parent / guardian: ....

Please allow 28 days for delivery. Offer is only available while stocks last. We reserve the right to change the terms of this offer at any time and we offer a 14 day money back guarantee. This does not affect your statutory rights. Offers apply to UK only.

☐ We may occasionally wish to send you information about other Egmont children's books.
If you would rather we didn't, please tick this box.

Ref: MRM 001